Sarah
and the
colorful Ghost

Ron Leunissen

ISBN 978-90-826174-3-6 by Ziva uitgeverij, Netherlands
Original title in Dutch: Sarah en het kleurenspook
English translation: Ron Leunissen, Mariana Funes

Sarah

and the
Colorful Ghost

Ron Leunissen

It's night.
The downstairs clock strikes one.
Everybody is asleep.
Everybody … except Sarah.
She just can't get to sleep.

Ugh! Still awake! Thinks Sarah.
I am bored.
I wish it were already morning.
Then I could get up.

Sarah has an idea.
What if I tell myself a story?
Then I could tell it to the other kids at school.
And, I may fall asleep while telling it.

So, Sarah starts to tell herself a story.
She makes it up as she goes along ...

'It is in the middle of the night.
It is storming outside.
Raindrops fall hard against
the window.
A girl is sitting on her bed.
Alone in a big house.'

Sarah hears a sudden thud.
She stops telling herself the story.
She gets out of the bed and closes
the door of the bedroom.

She gets back into bed and continues her story.

'The girl hears a thump on the corridor.
Scary!
She gets up quickly and closes the door
to the corridor but ...
It's too late!
A ghost comes floating in.
A black cloud with dark eyes floats
into the bedroom.'

Sarah shies away from the ghost. Oh no!
This story is getting way too scary.
I don't want such an eerie ghost in my story.
What shall I do?

'By the power of the girl's push, the ghost starts to disappear ...
Slowly the black cloud dissolves.'

This is going the right way, Sarah thinks.
This is less scary.

Yes, but ... says the ghost,
I am not really scary, I am a ...

'As it speaks, a big tear appears on the ghost's face. It hangs still in the air for a moment, and then ...'

'The tear begins to fall.
First slowly. Then faster and faster.
Until it falls on the ground.
Hundreds of tears with wonderful colors
appear. They fly around the bedroom,
like a moving rainbow'

beautiful

Sarah enjoys the beautiful colors.
The bedroom changes color again and again.
Like silent fireworks.
It seems to go on forever.

The ghost is no dark cloud anymore.
It has become a COLORFUL GHOST!
Sarah doesn't know what to look at
first. There are so many amazing colors
in the room.

It is late! says the ghost.
I have to go now. Shall I come back tomorrow?

'Yes,' Sarah answers excited.

amazing!

Okay, I will be back tomorrow, says the ghost. Tomorrow at the same time.

Slowly, the colorful ghost floats out the door.

But Sarah does not hear the ghost leave.
She now sleeps and dreams of her colorful ghost.